MW00463345

HAND IN HAND

By Tauno Yliruusi

Translated from the Finnish
with an Introduction by
Richard Impola

PAUL S. ERIKSSON *Publisher*
Middlebury　　　　　Vermont

10 9 8 7 6 5 4 3 2 1

Library of Congress Cataloging-in-Publication Data

Yliruusi, Tauno, 1927–
    [Käsi kädessä. English]
    Hand in hand / by Tauno Yliruusi ; translated from
the Finnish by Richard Impola.
        p.   cm.
    Translation of: Käsi kädessä.
    ISBN 0-8397-3156-6 : 17.95
    I. Title.
PH355.Y4K3713   1992
894'.54133--dc20   92–14603
                                                   CIP

Jacket and book design by Phyllis Demong

TO MY WIFE

INTRODUCTION

Among other things, *Hand in Hand* is a remarkable love story, not the usual tale of two beautiful young lovers, but the story of two aging people and their love's triumph over a dilemma increasingly prevalent in our time.

We all know the tragic tales of star-crossed lovers. They are young, for the intensity of love seems more fitting in them. Their capacity for idealizing a loved one makes their tragedy all the more poignant. And being completely wrapped up in each other, they are open to the chances and accidents that fate deals out.

The unspoken consolation in this is that love cut off in full bloom is perfect love. It can never fade. George Bernard Shaw, for one, was well aware of that when in *Candida*, he has the poet give up the woman he has been trying to woo away from her stodgy husband, knowing that romantic love is better fitted to survive as a poetic ideal than as a handmaid to domesticity. And perhaps current divorce rates underline that point.

Which suggests that love and marriage, contrary to the words of the popular song, don't go together. The only way to go from the heights of love is down. The phrase used by Millamant in Congreve's "The Way of the World," is perfectly apt. Given the right conditions, she may agree to "dwindle into a wife."

Is it possible to write a love story which departs from this pattern, but is still equally moving? Can the story of an aging couple whose love is so great that they cannot endure the thought of separation by death stand comparison with the great love stories? The test lies in the reading.

There is a great love story in which the characters are not the typical young lovers: Shakespeare's *Antony and Cleopatra*. But in that play, the love story is enhanced by being acted out against the clashing of armies and the crumbling of empires. Antony and Cleopatra are an incomparable pair. *Hand in Hand* in contrast, is about two rather prosaic older people, a retired civil servant and his wife.

The reason for the author's choice of such a couple may well lie in the strong realistic tradition among Finnish writers. There is even a name for it: domestic realism. Whatever the theme of a work — in this case a dual one: two-thirds of the great poetic trilogy of love, life, and death — it is likely to be developed through stories of quite ordinary human beings. In that sense, Finns are among the most democratic of writers; they see no need for Roman generals and Egyptian queens to dignify their works.

Perhaps the life of Thor and Anni is too idyllic for some people's notion of realism, but carefully presented, they come through as a believable pair. They are the ideal retired couple living in a little world of their own — their perfect apartment, their first real home. They are childless, their lives completely taken up with one another.

Realism implies relevance to social

issues of our time. It is a fact that our populations are growing older. In telling how he came to write this novel, the author, Tauno Yliruusi, says it began with a feeling that older people often suffer needlessly before dying. In writing about the subject, he follows a familiar pattern among Finnish writers: a larger social issue becomes a moving human story as it is experienced in the lives of Thor and Anni. That may be why Finland is a nation of readers, and why fiction is so highly regarded.

If the method works — and the reader is the final judge of that — it should be easier to identify with Thor and Anni than with the great lovers of legend. After all, the two are more like us. It is fascinating to watch the familiar cliches of love poetry become fresh and new in this story. The romantic notion that lovers become one takes on new meaning in the account of two lives so blended that "apart from one another they could not really be said to exist." The familiar idea that the outside world cannot understand lovers appears in the efforts of the physician to offer conventional consolations that mean nothing to Thor. The phrase "I can't live without you," is transformed from trite to profoundly moving in the whole action of the story. " 'Tis better to have loved and lost . . ." is turned inside out in the bitter comments on the advantages of never having developed close attachments. Whether a reader sees this as a love story or a comment on the universal human predicament, it is difficult to imagine a person who will not be moved by the power of the writing.

Richard Impola

HAND
IN
HAND

*SEE IN MY YARD
THERE IS A TREE.
IT ALWAYS BLOOMS IN
JUNE.*

I

Having heard in the hospital just what he had been afraid of hearing, that his wife was dying, Thor Helander, the former head of the market town employment agency, was on his way home in a bus.

The trip from Helsinki took nearly an hour and a half. Thor sat in the rear of the bus with his hat on his lap, his lips working in their habitual way. He looked as if he were always sucking on a caramel, although he never touched candy. He was a small and frail old man. All the driver could see of him when he looked at his passengers in the rear-view mirror were a head of gray hair combed forward and curling up over his ears, and small, reddish cheeks. His ruddy color, which made him look healthy, was the result of broken capillaries.

When the bus reached the town station, Thor put on his hat. He was the last to leave the bus. The driver nodded, smiling as Thor handed the small white slip back to him.

Thor and his wife Anni's apartment was in the very center of town, in a four-story co-op apartment house beside the market square. It was only some two hundred meters from the bus station. They had bought it fifteen years ago when the building was constructed.

"I'm not moving from here again, except to the grave," Thor had vowed when the furniture and other gear were properly installed.

They were both proud of their apartment, which had a roomy kitchen and bath in addition to the living room and bedroom. It was their first very own lodging. Before that, they had always rented. Not that they couldn't have afforded to buy, but they'd always happened to have suitable quarters that went with a job or an inexpensive place to rent. They had lived in at least ten different places before the much talked- and dreamt-about place of their own had materialized. But better late than never. Tenderly, lovingly, they had furnished and kept up the apartment, speaking of it to each other as warmly and enthusiastically as if it were a living human being. They could seldom stand to be away for a long time; a day or two of absence kindled an unbearable homesickness in them. Those who have children or other close relatives probably find such an attachment hard to understand. Or even a dog or cat. But Thor and Anni had only each other. And the apartment.

Thor stopped in the center of the market square and looked up at the familiar windows and the balcony on the third floor. The whole rim of the balcony was covered with flowers. There were red curtains on the kitchen window and white ones in the living room. Anni had sewn them herself, and when they were hung in the spring, the two of them had often gone out to the market square to see how they looked, both when the rooms were dark and when all the lights were on. They had looked fine under all conditions, even when only a floor lamp was burning in the living room. Not only he and Anni, but others as well, were of the opinion that the flowers on their balcony were the most beautiful and thriving in the whole house. They had flowers of three colors: white and blue petunias and red hanging begonias. Many other balconies had only one color. The fact that their flowers grew and bloomed so profusely was the result of Anni's tender care and above all, of her knowing enough to mix large amounts of peat moss into the soil.

For a long time, Thor stood in the empty, sunlit market square in his faded poplin coat and hat one size too big, looking up at the balcony and the curtains of his home, upon which the warm afternoon sun shone directly. He could not go any nearer, but stopped and raised his hands to his lips as if to stop their silent movement. Now and then an automobile drove by their house along Commerce Street. A few people walked along the street. A woman and her children entered the shoe store on the corner. It was the last of August, one of the warmest and loveliest days of the summer.

He looked around helplessly, not knowing what to do. Then he started off toward the bus station again, but seeing the station clock, he stopped, stood still for awhile, and put his hand to his mouth. No, that wasn't right, he shouldn't go that way. Some other way, any way at all. He went back a few steps and turned onto broad, maple-lined Park Road, which led to the shore.

The whole time since he had left the hospital, he had gone over in his mind the discussion with the young doctor in the white coat.

"I'm sorry, really sorry."

"Then you didn't operate on her?"

"Yes. Or rather no. We tried to. But unfortunately it had spread so far that . . . that we could do nothing."

"Nothing?"

"Nothing."

"But isn't there some way . . ."

"I'm really sorry, but I have to tell you that there isn't."

"Can you tell me, doctor, how long, how much time . . . ?"

"Maybe half a year. At most, half a year. Possibly not that long. I know how you feel now. It's a shock. It feels like the end of everything, as if life stopped here. But you can stand it. It's something we all have to face, sooner or later. Believe me, even the greatest grief has an end. It's hard at first, but then it gets easier. Every day it's a little easier. Be brave. Promise me. That's good. You'll come to see her often, won't you? Six months is a long time. Even a month is a long time. Try to think, to be thankful for every day you still have her. Make the time she has left as happy and as beautiful as possible. Won't you? Come and see her tomorrow. Act just as usual. Talk about everything imaginable except illness. Don't let her notice. It's better if she doesn't know."

It was a little cooler walking under the maples. Thor could already see the shore and the dock with motorboats tied to it, the familiar beach pavilion. A spasm of pain seized the middle of his chest. He stopped, took a small glass vial from his pocket, shook a red pill into one hand and thrust it into his mouth. By then his stopping had caused the sharp pain to subside; a heart muscle damaged by three blood clots had gotten enough blood.

Six months ago, after his last attack, the town physician had said to him:

"Avoid excitement, my good man, and any emotional stress. Even television is dangerous. I positively forbid your watching suspense films and sporting events. And try to cut down a little on smoking. A drink now and then doesn't hurt, but nicotine is poison."

The physician obviously knew what he was talking about. He was himself a chain-smoker.

Reaching the shore, Thor sat down

on a badly decaying bench near the beach pavilion, which had once been a café and later a dance hall. He and Anni had often sat there on warm summer nights looking at the lake, across whose surface the setting sun beyond Broad Point drew a long band of gold.

"Isn't it a gorgeous sight?" Anni had often asked. "Just look at it and enjoy it."

"It's really nice," Thor had usually answered.

On those evenings, watching as the red-hued sun sank slowly out of sight, to rise warm and golden a few hours later on the other horizon, the two of them had ruled over the beauty of life and the world. Satisfaction and quiet exultation had filled their hearts.

Now Thor watched as two young people, one of whom he recognized, untied a motorboat rope from the iron ring to which it was attached. The pair leaped lightly on board, the motor sputtered, and soon the brown craft was far out on the lake.

Scarcely aware of having smoked two consecutive cigarettes, Thor got up from the bench and hesitated, not knowing which way to go. He had to go somewhere; he couldn't just stay here. I have to go home, he thought. I can't go anywhere else. I have to go home.

He set out slowly, staring straight ahead, yet when he reached the market square, he did not cross it. Instead he went along Market to Commerce Street.

Be brave, the doctor had said. It's hard at first, but then it gets easier. Every day it's a little easier.

He did not see the people who

passed by him. He entered the lobby and rode the elevator to the third floor. Their apartment was the farthest to the right. He went to the door, took out his key, and inserted it into the lock.

The foyer was quiet, much quieter than when he had left for Helsinki in the morning. He took off his poplin coat slowly and hung it on the coat rack next to Anni's ulster. Then he took off his hat, set it on top of the rack, and went into the living room.

In the doorway, he stopped and stood still. He could see the bookshelf, the easy chairs, the white vase on a window sill, the small sculpture of a nude woman atop a cabinet, the graceful sofa that seated two, upholstered in a bluish-gray flower print. The sliding door to the kitchen was half open. Inside he could see a table with a red cloth, two sturdy chairs, a small gilt samovar, red curtains, some of the antique dishes suspended from the beige wall. On the table was a wicker basket of oranges.

Everything was the same — beautiful, clean, in good taste. But yet nothing was the same. There was no sound of steps in the kitchen, no clatter of dishes, no sound of cabinet doors opening and closing. No one was running water in the bathtub, no one coming from the bedroom with a dust cloth or newspaper in her hand, saying, "So you're here already? What is the weather like?"

Only a strange and crushing silence. Emptiness. Lack of movement.

Home seemed unreal and strange to Thor. Or rather, it no longer existed. Without Anni, there was no home, merely cold walls and doors, a collection of lifeless objects and household utensils, regarding him with cold restraint, almost as if he were an alien intruder. Only Anni's presence, her steps, voice, the touch of her hand could awaken them to life, make them familiar and friendly.

Thor went into the kitchen and drank a half glass of water. The door to one of the upper cabinets was ajar. He pushed it shut, went back into the living room, and sat down in an easy chair. On a table nearby were brochures from a travel agency. The cover of the topmost one had a picture of happy, tanned people at the shore. They had planned a trip to Majorca and had been to a passport photographer just two days before Anni fainted and was taken to the hospital.

It was to have been Anni's first voyage overseas.

"How can I leave our home for two weeks?" Anni had sighed, but she had looked forward to the trip with as much enthusiasm as Thor. They had both been sure that it would do her good, would restore her health. Furthermore, Anni would finally derive some benefit from her language skills. She had some knowledge — much better than Thor's — of both English and German.

On the very morning of the day she had been taken to the hospital, she had still been studying English.

"Oh, I've forgotten so much," she said. "Will I be able to speak English at all?"

To which Thor had replied with a wink.

"If anyone can, you can. You can interpret for me too when we go to a restaurant."

The slanting rays of the sun shone through the white curtains and lighted up the cabinet with the sculpture, throwing its shadow on the wall.

Thor rose and went into the bedroom. It was dark in there, the curtains tightly drawn. The sun shone there only in the early morning. The beds were pushed together, with a reading lamp affixed to the wall above each one. Small lace doilies were on the night tables. A white shag rug on the floor, a basket chair, and on the wall opposite the beds, a table made from an old sewing machine, painted white and with an opaque plate-glass top cover. On it were a small silver case, a blue glass bird, and an ornate hand mirror. On the wall above the table was a round mirror with a gilt frame.

The bed next to the window was

untouched. Thor sat on his own bed, which had been left unmade that morning. He lay on one side with his feet drawn up and took hold of Anni's pillow, drawing it up to his face.

"Anni . . ." he cried out. "Anni, dear Anni . . . my Anni . . . I can't stand this . . . I can't stand it . . ."

In his heart's panic, he kept babbling her name until the tears came and eased his suffocating grief for a while.

II

The following day Thor bought ten carnations from the Market Street florist, took the bus, and rode to Helsinki.

I must be calm, he kept repeating to himself as he sat in the rear of the bus with the flowers and his hat in his lap. Anni must not notice anything, I must be completely calm. I have to smile and make jokes.

But the closer he drew to Helsinki, the hospital, and Anni, the more pressure he felt. Now and then a lump rose in his throat and his eyes grew moist. Memories flickered through his mind . . . little everyday happenings, quiet moments at home in the evening before the television set, walking the streets of town together, the first visit to the travel agency. He remembered Anni's cheerful laugh, the sound of her steps in the kitchen, of the vacuum cleaner on the living room floor.

I can't start to cry, he thought. My voice mustn't shake. I have to be natural, just as before. I have to smile, make jokes. Otherwise Anni will notice.

Thor's chest began to hurt and tears dimmed his eyes. He felt so bad, so very bad. How could he ever go through with it. I won't go, he thought, panic-stricken. I won't go at all. I'll take the next bus back. Not 'til tomorrow, or the day after, when I'm calmer. Or would a drink help? It would calm him down, his voice wouldn't start shaking. What if he went to a restaurant first?

The thought of a restaurant made him feel a little better. When the bus arrived in Helsinki, there was still nearly an hour left 'til visiting time, easily enough to stop in at one.

Thor drank three brandies. Taken on an empty stomach — he had eaten nothing for twenty-four hours — they affected him quickly. The worst pain eased. He arrived at the hospital in a relatively brave state of mind.

Having left his outer wear at the checkroom in the lower lobby, he bought a chocolate bar in the canteen, rode the elevator to the fourteenth floor, and walked along the corridor to a set of large double doors.

They were a familiar sight. Before the operation, Thor had been here every day. But it was all so different. Although he had been more distraught for Anni's sake each time and deep down had feared the worst, there had always been hope.

But now that was gone.

He knocked cautiously and entered. There were eight beds in the room, four on either side, but Thor saw only Anni, who smiled and waved to him from the last bed.

Thor walked over to her and tried to twist his lips into a smile.

"Hi!"

"Well, hi. How are things?"

"So-so. I brought some flowers."

"Oh my, thanks. They're beautiful. Put them somewhere, even on the window sill. The nurse will get a vase for them."

Thor took the flowers over to the window.

"Get that chair and sit near me."

Thor took the chair from the foot of the bed, moved it close to Anni, and sat down.

"I even brought some chocolate," he said.

"My goodness, you'll spoil me completely. You open it."

Thor opened the paper at one end of the chocolate bar.

"I bought it from the canteen downstairs. Have some."

Anni broke off a small piece of chocolate and put it into her mouth.

"Thank you, my very own dear one," she said. "It is delicious. You take some."

"I don't care for chocolate," answered Thor, a little put out. He was afraid others had heard Anni call him her "very own dear one."

Thor could hear a quiet whispering and a rustle of paper behind him. When he turned around to look, he saw that at least four of the patients had visitors. Many people, children among them, were gathered around one of the beds.

Anni caught him by the hand.

"How have you really been getting along out there?"

"Perfectly well."

"Are you eating properly?"

"I am. All I need."

"I'm always afraid you won't get enough to eat when I'm here. I'm so silly."

"Well, you really are being silly now. One can get food from a store. People don't die of hunger nowadays."

"That's true. I'm so silly. I keep imagining that my Thor is sitting

there by himself hungry and lonesome. You must eat at a restaurant. At
least one proper meal a day. Do you
promise?"

"I do," Thor nodded. "To tell the
truth, I even stopped at a restaurant
today. On my way here. I had a couple
of drinks."

Anni squeezed his hand with a
smile.

"I noticed."

"How?"

"How would one notice? But have
your drink, as long as you remember
to eat first. Never on an empty stomach — isn't that right?"

"Agreed."

"And when I get home from here,
I'll make you a really delicious steak
again."

"Yes."

Anni closed her eyes. Talking had

sapped her strength. Weariness over-powered her, but it was good to lie with her hand in her husband's.

"Are you tired?" Thor whispered.

"A little," Anni mumbled. She had fallen asleep for a second. "I'm still a little groggy from drugs. Please forgive me, my own dear one, if . . ."

"Just go to sleep."

Anni had already dozed off. She had pulled Thor's hand against her cheek and slept breathing deeply. After a minute or two she opened her eyes and said with a smile:

"Hi."

"Hi," said Thor.

"Did I sleep?"

"You did. Just rest quietly."

"It passed over now. I feel com-pletely refreshed. It must be the anes-thetic and all the medications."

"It must be. You look a lot better

than last time," said Thor, and really meant it. Anni looked actually beautiful with her clear skin and dark brown hair with the many strands of gray running through it. It was hard to believe that she was sixty-five years old; in Thor's eyes, she looked thirty-five. It was even harder to believe that she would die, that at most she had only six months to live. For she looked much stronger now than when she had entered the hospital.

"Is it really true?" Anni was overjoyed. "But do you know the first thing I'm going to do when I leave here? I'm going to the hairdresser."

"But I think your hair is perfectly fine," Thor said.

"Oh my, it really needs to be set. I just tried to comb it a little before you came. Has the building super's wife been in?"

"She has. Just lately. The other day, or the day before that."

"Well, that's good. Did she water the flowers?"

"She did. Everything is under control."

"My very own dear."

"What?"

"Nothing. I just think it's so wonderful that you're here. That I can look at you. Thor . . . "

"Yes?"

"Have you missed me at all?"

"I have."

"I missed you too." Anni's eyes misted over, and she wiped them with the back of her hand. "So terribly. Oh Thor, my own Thor."

"You mustn't cry."

"I'm not crying. I'm just so happy you're here. Kiss me once."

Thor looked around, leaned over,

and kissed her lips. Anni patted his cheek with her hand.

"Once more."

Thor kissed her again. Her lips felt hot and dry.

"My very own," Anni whispered.

"And you too."

"Am I?"

"You are."

"So I am," Anni smiled. "Your very own Anni. But you haven't lost weight?"

"No."

"But now when I look at you, I see that you have. It's very plain."

"Well, maybe a little. But it's good for the heart."

"Yes, but you're already so thin you can't afford to lose. Remember now to eat in a restaurant every day. You must promise me."

"I promise."

"Your thumb on it?"

"My thumb on it."

They pressed their thumbs against each other's. It was their way of sealing promises which were not always easy for Thor to keep. But sometimes the seal stayed unbroken.

"Have you felt anything in your heart?" asked Anni.

"No."

"Well, that's good. Remember always to keep the pills with you."

Thor took a glass vial from his pocket and showed it to Anni.

"Good," said Anni. "And remember, no exertion or late hours. And not too many drinks, either."

"No."

"And not too much smoking. Remember what the doctor said." Anni's expression of concern dissolved into a smile. "Oh Thor, my love. I'm preaching to you again. Am I completely impossible?"

"No, you're absolutely right. And I have cut down on smoking."

"Have you?"

"Very appreciably. Today I've smoked only three . . . or four."

His memory had deceived him a little on this point. He had smoked at least five in the restaurant alone.

"You don't know how happy you make me," Anni whispered. A heavy weariness overcame her again, and she was forced to close her eyes.

Thor held her hand and let her sleep. When visiting hours were over, he whispered:

"I'll see you again, Anni. I have to go now."

Anni opened her eyes, apparently unaware that she had been asleep.

"Is it so late already?"

"It is, everyone has left. I'll come again tomorrow."

"Come tomorrow, dear," Anni mumbled. "I'll probably sleep a little."

"Just go to sleep." Thor let go of Anni's hand carefully and pulled the cover more completely over her. "Goodbye," he whispered.

Anni was already sound asleep.

Thor rose and walked cautiously across the room. The nurse who had entered nodded with a smile of sympathy as he bowed to her in an old-fashioned gentleman's way before going out the door.

III

Thor awoke at eight and groped at the bed beside his. He had dreamt that Anni was sleeping there. But the bed was empty. His hand touched only the smooth bedspread. Everything came back to him; the few hours of oblivion afforded by sleep were over.

He put on his slippers and went into the living room to get a cigarette. It tasted foul. His stomach felt pinched and empty. He should make tea, he thought. He should eat something.

Having dressed, he did go into the kitchen, but there he felt completely helpless. It was Anni's world, strange and unknown to Thor. Every day he had seen her bustling about in the kitchen, preparing food, making tea, taking dishes from the cupboard — it had all seemed so simple and easy. Where should he begin, he wondered. What kind of kettle is used for brewing tea? He opened door after door of the cabinets, but kettles and teacups seemed to hide from him, to be mocking him. There were plates and glasses aplenty, flour, sugar, and sauce jars in one of the cupboards, but where were all the kettles? Thor remembered vaguely that Anni had made tea in a small red kettle. It must be somewhere. Why did there have to be so awfully many cupboards. There were even some on the other side of the kitchen opposite the counter. He opened the topmost cupboards. They were full of glassware, Anni's antique stemware, goblets, and decanters. On one shelf was a fine set of china he did not remember ever having seen. And the lower cupboards? A pressing iron, a drawer of string, clothespins, shoe-polishing gear, a small red watering can. Everything neat and in good order.

At last Thor found a kettle, not the one he was looking for, but still a kettle. It was behind a frying pan in the cupboard below the refrigerator — a large, bluish-gray three-liter kettle. But he could not find the tea bags anywhere. We're probably out of them, he thought. Should he go to the store? There was a container half full of sour milk in the refrigerator. He emptied it into the sink. Should I go to the store and buy some tea bags, he wondered. And some milk and a loaf of French bread. Then I could make tea and eat a couple of slices of French bread. Maybe a little sausage too. Made from wild game. And eggs. Six eggs in a container. He could eat them during the day. They would be easy to cook.

He went into the hallway, put on his hat, took Anni's brown shopping bag from the rack, and went out.

And what if they start to ask questions? he thought as he stepped out onto the sunny street. How is your wife? When is she getting out of the hospital? I don't have to answer. I'll just buy a liter of milk and a loaf of French bread. And sausage and six eggs.

The store was on the next corner.

Thor felt as if the people walking by were looking at him sympathetically. Did everyone already know? A woman who looked familiar nodded to him, stopped as if she were about to ask him something, but then went on her way. Some friend of Anni's. Thor remembered having seen her in their home.

Thor reached the store. He stopped in front of the large display window and looked at the produce and the canned goods. There were several customers inside. A clerk came to get a bunch of bananas from the window. She noticed Thor, smiled through the window, and left with her bananas.

I'll go to another store, he thought. He started to walk back. Reaching the door of his home he stopped and looked for awhile at the market, with its parked cars.

He went back into the house with the empty shopping bag, heated some water, and drank it from a glass with some sugar in it.

IV

he building super's wife came at nine-thirty. She was a stout young woman.

"Good day," she said and went straight to the cleaning closet in the hallway and dragged the vacuum cleaner into the living room. She worked as knowledgeably and decisively as if she were in her own apartment. Thor had to move out of her way many times. He went to sit down at the kitchen table and watched the woman's activity from there. It seemed sad that a strange woman was fussing around Anni's home that way, touching her furniture and goods. It was wrong. Only Anni had the right to do it. At least Anni should be watching, telling her what to do and how. But Anni lay in the hospital, helpless and unable to defend herself.

After vacuuming the living room floor and the tops of the furniture, the woman moved into the bedroom. He could hear her shaking the bed-clothes. She didn't have to make the bed, Thor said to himself. Then the hum of the vacuum cleaner began. From time to time there were bump-ing and scraping sounds. She's denting the legs of the bed, thought Thor.

"How's your wife?" asked the woman as she came out of the bedroom.

"She's fine."

"That's nice."

The woman took the vacuum cleaner back to the closet and came into the kitchen. She washed the glass and kettle and put them on the drying rack. Having wiped the counter till it shone, she went to dust the living room furniture. Finished with that, she fussed about the bathroom for awhile, came back into the kitchen, took a watering can from the bottom cupboard, filled it with water and went out on the balcony to water the flowers.

"How much do I owe you?" asked Thor when she was finished.

"Your wife will pay me later," said the woman. "I'll wash the windows next time."

"That's not necessary."

"Your wife said to."

"Oh."

"Should I go to the store?"

"It's not necessary."

"I'll see you then. I'll be back on Monday."

"Goodby."

The woman left.

Thor went to the window and looked out at the market place. He had often stood there and waited for Anni to appear on Market Street and cross the square on her way home. She had always taken that route on her way from the Workers' School or the library.

Even now he was waiting for Anni, as senseless as that might be. When all hope is gone, a person expects a miracle. He stared at the farthest corner of the square, where there was a gas station, and imagined that Anni would appear from behind it, as she had so often before, and walk across the square. And when a woman who somewhat resembled her did suddenly come into view in the square, a great surge of joy swept through his heart before his brain could tell him that the woman could not be Anni, that Anni was lying in the hospital. But nevertheless he kept on waiting, staring closely at every woman he saw, hoping that it was Anni, that the doctors had realized their mistake, that a healthy and happy Anni would return home along the familiar route.

For a long time he stood at the window staring at the market square, waiting for a miracle he did not believe in.

At eleven he went out, ate a frankfurter at the gas station lunch counter, bought some flowers, and walked to the bus station, where he took the 11:45 bus.

V

After returning from Helsinki that evening and spending two long hours at home, Thor went to a restaurant. It belonged to the cooperative and was the only one in town that was fully licensed.

"Welcome," said the cloakroom attendant, taking his hat and poplin coat. He was pleased that at least someone wore outer clothing in the summer. There was only one hat on the rack.

"Thank you," said Thor.

"You're welcome," said the attendant, handing him the check.

"Thank you."

Thor put the coat check into his breast pocket. He flashed a shy smile at the attendant, patted his pockets, and walked to the restaurant door where he stood for a moment touching his mouth and looking into the room. Then he walked to his regular table near a column. He always sat there.

It was quiet in the restaurant. Only three of the tables had customers. Thor recognized them all.

The waitress arrived, a thin, pallid woman. She looked harassed, but she was friendly. Thor ordered a brandy and a cutlet. He wasn't hungry, but Anni had reminded him again about eating. On leaving home, he had planned on having two brandies first. Perhaps the food would taste good then.

"You can bring me another like this before the food," he said when the waitress set down the glass and poured soda water into it.

"There's plenty of time," said the waitress. "The cutlet will take awhile."

"There's no hurry," said Thor, having decided to have a third brandy before dinner.

Often before this, Thor had thought of dying, pondered its mysteries, declared his opinions both drunk and sober. As a young man, he had regarded it boldly and arrogantly, as one does a thunderstorm or any danger which exists in theory but is an unlikely possibility, which is far away, at a safe distance. Then it had been easy to say, "It'll nab you one of these days," or "Death is as natural as birth; there's nothing strange or terrifying about it." But every year had brought the danger a little closer and at the same time made it a little more strange and terrifying. The further away one got from birth, that natural beginning, the more incomprehensible did the end and its inevitability become. It was not nearly as natural an event as it had seemed in youth, not nearly as self-evident and proper. Not one's own death, nor that of a near and dear person.

As Thor sipped the brandy and thought about the death sentence imposed on his wife, it seemed completely unnatural, irrationally wrong, and incomprehensibly cruel. It was an injustice to both of them, a horrifying crime against their humanity. Thor did admit the inevitability of death in life's eternal cycle; he was fully aware that without death there could be no life, that they were the precondition and the consequence of each other. He was protesting not against death itself, but against the methods it employed, against its separating without pity or remorse two people whose lives had grown together.

Thor and Anni had been married for forty-three years. Happily married. Not that they hadn't had difficult conflicts, mutual jealousy, domestic quarrels in which both dishes and furniture had been broken, days on end of sulking, times when they hated rather than loved each other. There had been bitter disappointments and adversities, even sorrows, for their only child had been stillborn.

But everything negative had long since dissolved into the positive, making it stronger and more lasting in every way. Having shed the worst of selfishness, they had learned — or, so to speak, got the habit — not only of loving and admiring, but also of respecting and esteeming each other, because of which their physical love-life, which had continued regularly until Anni fell ill, had been lively and subtly nuanced.

Because Thor and Anni had only one another, their unity was strengthened. Each knew the other through and through, knew what the other thought or intended to say before it was said. Their thoughts, their souls, their whole world of experience were bound together with so many fibers that apart from one another they could not really be said to exist. Only together, within sight or hearing, did they become integral and whole.

How was it possible that this common life, this harmonious whole could suddenly be shattered, shamed, trampled to the ground? How was it possible for a happy marriage that had lasted forty-three years to end in a dismal catastrophe?

Both Thor's mind and his feelings refused to approve this ending. It was a senseless, incomprehensible ending to a life which had held so much that was beautiful, worthwhile, and good. It was totally unrelated to the years they had lived, to anything at all. What did love, devotion, rich years spent together mean if it all ended with their being wrenched apart just when they would have most needed each other, hurled to death in misery far from one another. To die in loneliness, pain, and oppression. What sense was there in life that shamed and negated one so horribly in a moment? Were the lived years of happiness any compensation for what death destroyed? Didn't death, in its incomprehensible cruelty, render null and void, like a fleeting dream, everything that had preceded it? When the end is good, all is good, says the proverb. And when the end is bad? Isn't everything else bad then? Only the end meant anything, only the end assigned a thing its final value and significance. When the end is good, everything is good. When the end is bad, everything is bad.

A helpless bitterness, which brandy could not alleviate, filled Thor's mind. He saw his entire life and marriage as a wretched deceit, a misleading delusion which had beguiled him from day to day 'til the moment when the truth was at last revealed in all its grinning horror, when life, which had appeared so beautiful and enticing revealed its true face — its monstrous face — mocking and sneering at his good faith and trust.

The thought that Anni, his beloved Anni, would die alone in a hospital bed surrounded by strangers forced tears of torment and shame from Thor's eyes. It wasn't right. It couldn't be right. It was senseless, infuriating. He knew how alone and sorrowful Anni already was in the hospital without her husband and her beloved home. What about when the moment of departure came? Thor could visualize her fear and panic, her boundless loneliness and despair, life's final payment to Anni, one who had admired and revered it so faithfully.

Thor became indignant pondering these ultimate questions of life's deceit and death's cruelty. There was no sense — not to mention justice — in separating two people deeply attached to each other, after forty-three years of marriage, and subjecting them to inconsolable grief as if they were being punished for having led model lives.

Something must be fundamentally wrong when such things can happen, he thought. The most rudimentary sense of justice can understand that. No matter what the perspective, no matter how one studies the question, one can only conclude that a fundamental error has been made.

Perhaps it is in life itself, he mused bitterly. Perhaps life, this sweet and beautiful life with all its wonders, is a gigantic hoax, a series of unkept promises and lures with which trusting people, the clowns of existence, are enticed to the edge of the abyss.

But who profits from this scam? Who has devised it? Who laughs maliciously whenever some poor innocent realizes the deceit a moment before he or a dear one is thrown into the abyss?

Who enjoys all this?

God — that nice benevolent old gentleman?

It was hard to believe. All signs pointed to the devil, rather, who derives special joy from human misery, pain, and despair.

Of course, Thor reflected, a part of the fault may lie in man, in his slightly unnatural ability to think and feel at the same time. Perhaps his flaw was that, unlike other animals, he had learned to use his brain for reasoning. Undeniably that increased his knowledge, and Thor knew the adage that he who increases knowledge increases sorrow. For a human being is the only creature who knows in advance about death, which is the betrayal of life. He knows that everything ends in death. He senses a hoax even in childhood, although he pushes it from his mind, since life seems to have so much to offer. But the world of happy, trusting play, which other animals continue to the end of their lives, ends for him in early youth. He becomes serious and concerned, and in his despairing self-deceit he thinks it good. Before long, his unmade will begins to trouble his mind.

Or perhaps, Thor brooded, the fault is in both life and man. From man's point of view, life is obviously a shocking deceit, but only because man is capable of thought. The matter is otherwise with dumb animals, and here the saying that one pays a price for stupidity does not hold true.

But in any case, a man's lot cannot be considered enviable. Even wishful thinking cannot view as happy a life which ends miserably in death, no matter how great and fine it seems in anticipation or in retrospect. A catastrophe is always a catastrophe. When a ship's voyage — no matter how beautiful the weather, how happy the people, how pleasant and cheerful everything else may be — ends in a destructive shipwreck, it would take a confirmed cynic to call it a successful voyage.

Yes, Thor concluded, when the end is bad, everything is bad. An unfortunate truth, its sadness increased rather than diminished by the fact that one is so vividly aware of his own and his dear ones' bad end.

For many, as for him, the departure of a dear one was a greater problem than their own death, though an appreciable amount of the distress at the thought of dying lay in the grief and longing which they feared — rightly or wrongly — to leave behind. How much easier and simpler would death be if there were no near and dear ones, no mutual affection among people.

It was the final irony, he thought, that sorrow and grief themselves made death so completely without consolation. It wasn't enough for death to unmask the life of a human being as a wretched deceit by ending it forever, as if it had never been; it also seized the innocent victim's surviving relatives by the throat with its black hand, holding them in its choking grip for an unconscionably long time, sometimes to the very grave.

Of course, priests and psychologists,

those well-intentioned people, con-
sole others and themselves, assuring
them that sorrow is sure to end in
time, that each day is a little easier, as
the young doctor had said to him.
Certainly it was so. Otherwise the
world would overflow with weeping
and lamentation; everyone would be
overcome with grief, and life's cleverly
calculated deceit, in which forgetful-
ness plays a crucial role, would come
to naught. It is natural for time to
diminish grief, in some cases to elimi-
nate it entirely — life sees to that —
but that did not alter the case for him.
To him, death was and would remain
man's most fiendish, infuriating, and
shameful enemy. When something,
either a human agency or death itself,
separates from each other two loving
spouses who have been one for over
forty years, hurling them into a dark

gulf alone and far from each other, the inhumanity and callousness of the deed is so unspeakably vile and infuriating that only a lunatic would rise to defend it. And only the devil himself could see anything beautiful and sublime in it.

This tormented analysis only increased Thor's sense of shame and anger, and he tried to alleviate his bottomless grief with brandy. He had three drinks before he could even bring himself to taste the cutlet.

"Listen. Some day fifty years will have passed from today, and then we will no longer exist. Isn't it remarkable when you think about it? And that day will inevitably come, sooner or later."

They were his own words, spoken some thirty years ago. He remembered them clearly as he chewed on the cutlet. They had been in bed. It was evening, but death was not yet lurking in the corner, so they could discuss it naturally and without any great fear.

"I want to die before you," said Anni.

"Why?"

"I couldn't live alone without you."

"You might get married again."

"Now you're being stupid, Thor. You offend me."

"Forgive me, darling."

"I forgive you. But you mustn't ever say such things. Or even think them."

"But it's a medical fact that women live longer than men. According to statistics, you will live six years longer than I will."

"I won't."

"You will. It's a statistical probability."

"I don't believe your statistics."

"They're not my statistics."

"Darling, you are delightful."

"So are you. But let's agree that we'll die at the same time."

"Oh, if only it were possible."

"Like this. Together. Hand in hand."

"That would be beautiful."

"The proper way to die."

"Then I wouldn't be afraid to die."

"Are you afraid?"

"Sometimes. Are you?"

"Perhaps sometimes. All people are afraid to die. But that's only the instinct of self-preservation. The same instinct that makes a fly take off when your finger comes near it. Actually the fear of death is completely pointless."

"That way I wouldn't be at all afraid. I would be ready to die right now. If I could only be near you and hold your hand."

"Yes, it would really be no more than falling asleep. Except that one wouldn't wake up in the morning. But a person doesn't know when he falls asleep whether or not he'll wake up."

"No, he doesn't."

"And it's all the same to him whether he wakes up or not since he knows nothing about it."

"Yes, darling."

"We only imagine that we have to wake up every morning, go to work, and live one more day. But in the last analysis, is it necessary? It all stems from the instinct for self-preservation, which is a purely atavistic phenomenon. I think there's something idiotic about it."

"Why can't people die like this? Satisfied and happy."

"Because of the instinct for self-preservation. It has made such a dreadful matter of death that one's hair stands on end at the mere sound of the word. People just don't dare to die satisfied and happy."

"What a calamity that is."

"Undeniably. But on the other hand, it is quite understandable. Without an instinct for self-preservation, there would be no people. Or other life on this planet, for that matter."

Now thirty years had gone by since that discussion. Had it been a long or a short time? To Thor, it seemed only a year or two. He remembered everything so well, the tone of Anni's voice, her smile of quiet satisfaction as she lay beside him with her eyes closed. They were living in an apartment that went with the job, a large apartment. The bedroom was at least twice as big as their present one. It had green wallpaper, and a large clothes closet in one corner.

"Wasn't it good?" asked the waitress. She looked disappointed as she took away the plate with more than half the cutlet still on it.

"Really, it was good," said Thor. "The serving was just a little too large for a small man. But how would it be . . . if I had another brandy like this?"

After that, he ordered only two more. He staggered slightly when he rose from the table, but walked into the entry even more erect than when he had come in. Searching through his pockets for awhile, he found the coat check and gave it to the attendant.

"There it is," said the attendant, looking at the number from force of long habit before he took down Thor's poplin coat, the only one on the rack, and helped him on with it. "Well, it went a little wrong," he laughed, when one arm wouldn't go into a sleeve. "There now, that's right. And here's your hat."

Thor set his hat on his head and gave the attendant a *markka* he had held in his hand since getting up from the table.

"Thank you very much," said the attendant.

Thor stood there fingering his mouth. The attendant looked benevolently at this old customer who had had a couple of drinks more than usual.

"Yes?"

"Thank you," said Thor.

"My thanks to you," said the attendant. "Come back again."

Thor took a couple of steps toward the door and turned to look at the attendant.

"My wife is in the hospital."

"Is that so. It's too bad."

"For two weeks already."

"I hope it's nothing serious."

"No it isn't."

"That's good. She'll soon be home again."

"She will. So goodbye then."

The attendant hurried to open the door.

"Goodbye, goodbye. Come again. Give my regards to your wife."

"Thank you."

Thor stepped out a little uncertainly into the warm August twilight. The neon lights of businesses were already on, the first stars were beginning to shine in the clear sky, and young people were gathered at the street corners.

VI

nce again Thor had a terrible feeling of dread at the thought of going home to the empty apartment. He walked slowly, trying to postpone the awful moment. His mind was in a turmoil. How much better it would be, he thought, if mortal human beings did not grow too fond of each other, if we did not come to be as dependent on other people as we are wont to do. It is just this exceptional affection, tenderness, and love,

this being used to our lifetime com-
panion's constant presence, to her
thoughts, voice, and gestures, this
seeking and cherishing of common
memories, this sharing of an entire life
of joys and sorrows with another, as it
has been with Anni and me — it is all
this that puts the last trumps into
death's hand when the final and deci-
sive round of play begins. Our inevitable defeat is then sorrowful in the ex-
treme. Not just because we die twice
instead of only once, but because the
deception of life is bitterest for him
who seems to have gotten the most
from it and has therefore trusted the
most in it.

Thor came to the flower shop and
gazed absently at the colorful window
display. But his mind was with Anni,
his heart wrestling with the sad con-
tradictions of life. The ability to love,

to feel affection for another person, he thought, is a gift for which we have throughout time thanked its giver, life. It seems to offer a unique happiness, much joy, renewal, and pleasure, and a secure refuge from loneliness. Many to whom life has denied this gift weep over their harsh fate — without good cause. For when two people, such as Anni and me, are trustingly joined by the bonds of common experience, mutual respect, faith, and every sort of emotion, they gradually become one — they grow together like a grafted tree, and then the departure of one of them leaves behind only wretched fragments of what should have been a beautiful whole. Nothing of value is left, nothing that could have a positive significance. Only mute grief and longing, and sometimes a bad conscience, although forgetting — one of life's tools — sometimes, if there is sufficient time left, changes those feelings to "beautiful memories."

Thor thought about the many poets — from writers of folk songs to Finland's beloved Aleksis Kivi — who have more or less openly presented man's hope of dying alone and forgotten, separated from others, with no one to mourn or pine for him. And there are people who fear too strong attachments, as if avoiding them will undermine death's tyranny.

Life without Anni, he knew, would be unthinkably sad and lonesome. Tenderness and love, the longing for the proximity of another person — these too a gift of life — seem basic to human nature. But if one remained alone, so distant from friends and acquaintances that in dying they took

no piece of him along with them —
that was full recompense for what he
had missed. When the inevitable end
drew near, that man could mock at
sorrow. Understandably melancholy
but undeceived, he could give final
assent to the songwriter's words:

> There is one consolation:
> on my grave
> no tears will be shed.

In the depths of his grief, Thor
could see life only as deception. All
shared affection, love, and human
warmth were deception's tools, revealed as such when death with one
blow nullified and annihilated everything truly meaningful, everything
built and cherished over decades. To
him only one thing mattered — how
much of this, of his thoughts, feelings,

and affections, could death rob him of? Death was irrefutably man's worst enemy, but paradoxically man lived only to die. He journeyed toward death; it was his final destination, not only as an individual but as a species. Yet he must fight against it, try to diminish its power, deceive it. The possibilities were unusually limited, almost non-existent. He could not defeat death itself but only its mournful allies: sorrow, grief, and despair. Even the smallest victory over death's tyranny was worth so much that a man had full reason to congratulate a fellow human being who had managed to avoid excessive fondness for any living creature.

Well, there was a way of cheating death, its black allies and its malicious paid lackey, life. It was relatively exclusive in nature, possible only in a few cases and then under the most propitious circumstances. There was a way.

VII

hor had a chocolate bar with him when he went to see Anni again, but she no longer cared for chocolate. The previous bar lay almost untouched on her table. For Thor, it was a bad sign. Chocolate had always been a passion with Anni.

"Not even a little piece?"

"You're awfully nice but I'm afraid it won't agree with me."

"It'll make you strong."

Anni smiled. Thor's expression was

so concerned and appealing.

"Well all right then. But a very small piece. Half of that."

Thor broke the square of chocolate once more, giving the larger piece to Anni, and eating the smaller one himself.

"Thank you darling. It tastes good."

"It'll make you strong."

"Hold my hand," Anni asked.

"Like this?"

"Like that. That feels good."

They were silent for a long time, both thinking the same thought. Soft conversation could be heard from around the other beds. On the window sill in back of Anni's bed were four vases filled with flowers Thor had brought.

"Thor . . ."

Thor shifted his gaze from the flowers and met Anni's wondrously beautiful gaze.

"Yes?"

"Promise me something."

"I will. Anything at all."

"You mustn't mourn if I . . ."

"You can't say such things," Thor interrupted her, frightened. "Now you're being absolutely childish. You can't for a minute imagine such a thing. Promise me."

"Thor, love," Anni whispered, smiling.

"You can't even think such things. Not ever."

"My very own. Let me touch your cheek. My own Thor. My only one. We've always been honest with each other. Haven't we? I would like to be able to talk openly about everything, and about that too. It probably isn't what people say it is. And it comes to everybody some day. You can't avoid it. I don't want us to pretend to each other. It's not like us at all. Isn't that true? My Thor. Who else has such a smooth cheek? You've shaved with a new blade. Come a little closer so that I can smell your aftershave. I like it so much."

Thor rested his head on the pillow next to Anni. He no longer could, no longer even wanted to battle the choking pain that discharged itself in tears and sobs that shook his shoulders.

"My very own," Anni whispered, patting his cheek. "Don't cry, my most beloved. We're brave, both of us."

"Anni, Anni," Thor sobbed. "I feel so bad. I feel so bad."

"It will pass," Anni consoled him. "Keep your chin up, Thor. Let's not be stupid and gloomy, shall we? And I may even get better yet. Such things have happened before."

Thor raised his wet cheeks from the pillow.

"You have to get better. You have to. I can't live without you. I'll die if you . . ."

"No Thor. You'll live a long time yet."

"Why should I live if you die?"

"Because you have to live. You'll take care of our home, go for walks, and remember me sometimes, your own Anni. But let's not talk about sad things now. How are the flowers doing on the balcony? And has there been anything interesting in the mail? Tell me what the weather is like. Have you seen anyone we know?"

Thor left the hospital more sorrowful than ever. Anni knew the truth. It doubled Thor's grief, for they had long since become one.

It was three o'clock, the hottest part of the day. Only a couple of flimsy clouds looked at the capital from a blue sky, at its buildings, lush parks, and streets one side of which was constantly in the shade. A gorgeous day, lovely and warm, not a breeze stirring. Sailboats stood still on the sea, sun-worshippers lay languid on the sandy shore and on the crags of Rowan Island. They were as motionless as the leaves on the trees in the park. But the streets downtown swirled with animation, tanned people in bright summer clothing criss-crossed everywhere, some on their way home, some on their way to a beach or restaurant. There were cheerful, happy faces, smiles, easy laughter, but also sober, worried faces, haste, impatience. Automobiles, driven by men in shirt sleeves, traveled slower than usual, their windows cranked down as if merely seeking a shady place to park, and now and then sedate yellowish-green streetcars clattered along the street stopping the other traffic for a moment by right of seniority.

Thor, whose forehead was glistening with perspiration, took off his hat. It was too much on a day like this. The hospital had been cool and dim compared to the warm, bright outdoors.

Why should I live, if you die? Thor repeated this question to himself as he walked behind the Glass Palace toward the bus station. Twice he even said it aloud.

Why should I live, if you die?

Why? What meaning would life have with Anni dead? Thor knew that he himself had little time left. Perhaps a year or two, at most three or four.

What kind of years would they be? Empty, hopelessly empty and unnecessary, mere waiting for death, ceaseless longing, grief, and shame. Grief and shame at the helplessness of human beings, at Anni's having to go in such a way, at having everything end so wrongly, so wrongly.

Many oncomers, happy and sunburned people, whom the warm weather had caused to forget their own troubles and griefs, looked with a smile of sympathy at the little old gentleman who walked along hat in hand, wearing a faded poplin coat in the hot sunshine. They, of course, had no inkling of the kind of torment he bore in his heart; there was just something very moving and even amusing in the pleasant-looking, red-cheeked old man whose lips worked as if he were talking to himself.

Thor did not really notice the on-comers. The city to which he had wanted so eagerly to move with Anni some twenty years ago meant nothing to him, these people, buildings, shops, restaurants meant nothing. Nothing did. Not even his home town. Not even his own home. Without Anni, there was no home. Without Anni, there was nothing.

Why should I live, if you die?

The thought of his own life ending did not frighten Thor. He had had many chances to get used to the idea during his lifetime. Even the thought of doing it himself no longer seemed so terrible.

Only one thing frightened and hor-rified him: that Anni should die first, that they should be dragged apart from each other at the crucial, deci-sive moment.

Of what benefit would even suicide be then? The catastrophe would already have occurred, everything would have ended in torment, shame, and humiliation. What compensation could suicide offer then? Wouldn't it be just one more wretched and shameful end, another victory for sneering, mocking death?

No, one couldn't even fight death by dying. Evil is no help against evil. Unless it could happen at the same time, if there wasn't first one death and then another, but two simultaneous deaths, two deaths together.

Together . . . ?

Thor's sorrowful thoughts stopped at this word, it rushed through his mind like a sudden, surprising gust of wind through an oppressive calm.

Together. To die together. Side by side. Hand in hand. Was that it? Was that the solution to the problem for which there was no solution?

The confusion that overcame him was so great that he had to stop. An incredible, almost incomprehensible feeling of well-being flowed through him. Good Lord, was it possible? Why not? It had to be. It was the only possibility, the only solution. The only one. The only one. To die together, hand in hand. Without pain, without sorrow, without longing. Together. Exactly like going to sleep some night.

During the whole voyage home in the bus, Thor elaborated on the idea, examined it from one side and the other, posed questions to himself and answered them. The more he thought about it, the more assured he became of its justifiability, its all-around rationality, and of his having conceived of something tremendous, something that had seemed impossible to human beings: a way to deceive death and its black allies, a way to bring home a final victory.

This was not a question of a calcified old man's dim and irresponsible cerebral processes, of a capacity for understanding weakened by an overwhelming grief or of a state of depression comparable to mental derangement. In truth, Thor was relatively old and his heart was badly damaged, but he was far from old in his ability to think clearly. He was mentally vigorous, his brain worked flawlessly, he was responsible in the full meaning of the word, fully aware of his thoughts and deeds and their consequences. The grief and oppression he felt were indeed great, but hardly greater than that of anyone facing a death in the family. As to the idea that this mental distress and despair could have dimmed his comprehension, it seemed on the contrary to have clarified it, burned off everything irrelevant and insignificant, and helped him to reach the decision that seemed the only right one, the thought of which consoled him many times more than could the finest funeral service or the warmest words of consolation.

He could concede that the moral issue was open to discussion. He knew it was customary to regard a voluntary departure from life, whatever the motive, with a certain horror, to view it as even more to be condemned than killing another. The Christian Church had always held it to be a sin of the first magnitude, and present-day enlightened society, which had succeeded in freeing men from so many prejudices, still viewed it as a shocking human tragedy which one should do everything possible to prevent.

Yet he was convinced, in all honesty and objectivity, that a man could not think about ultimate questions and individual decisions with regard to them only from the viewpoint of self-preservation and its presuppositions. In the last analysis, it was wrong for man's lowest and most primitive levels alone to decide his relationship to morality, to decide what he should consider right, what wrong, what beautiful, what ugly, what worthy, what worthless, what a happy ending, what an inhuman tragedy. Especially when he had the clear possibility, at least under some conditions, of freeing himself from the control of his instincts in cases where human truth and value are involved and of getting at least a glimpse of other, perhaps higher, truths and values.

But whatever the morality and the esthetics of Thor's thought, its psychic and physiological effects on him were only positive. The smothering sensation that had lasted for days disappeared from his breast, and he was hungry.

VIII

When Thor was doing his morning shopping or walking along the street with his purchases, he sometimes met people who lived in the center of town, acquaintances and others he knew only by sight. When they stopped to exchange a word or two with him, they seemed slightly disappointed, as if they had been mistaken or led astray in believing that Anni, "the lady with the mink coat," had gone to the hospital for the last time.

Nonetheless everyone without exception tried carefully to conceal the disappointment, as if it were something unnatural and shameful. Yet nothing is more natural and understandable than that people who regard death with horror should feel a sense of satisfaction on hearing that an acquaintance or a person they know by name has died or is about to die. And a corresponding sense of disappointment if the news seems premature. The unspoken feeling of gratification which such a message of sorrow always brings with it is of the same atavistic origin as the sense of self-preservation which sees one's own or a dear one's departure as the end of the world. If there is something shameful in this, at least it is not a person's fault.

Thor was almost his former self. His

eyes, which had a tendency to mist up, regained their old twinkle. His wise, restrained smile played about his lips once more. His walk, which had been draggy for a few days and told people much about Anni's condition, again became his former spirited gait.

People thought it must mean that his wife was convalescing and would return home, that the pleasant couple would soon be seen out walking and shopping together. And when the first feeling of disappointment passed, many remarked to their spouses and acquaintances how good it was that everything seemed to have taken a turn for the better, that the woman who always smiled in such a friendly way, the one with the mink coat, was likely to be home from the hospital soon, that it probably wasn't anything serious after all.

"It certainly is a good thing," the townspeople repeated with a sigh. "They are such pleasant and well-educated people."

To those who did not want to trust to their eyes alone and whose curiosity emboldened them to ask about Anni's health, Thor answered:

"Everything is fine."

Nor was he lying. From his point of view, everything did seem to be well. His life had a clear and logical goal, and when he returned from shopping, he bustled about the kitchen as busily and enthusiastically, drank his tea and ate his sandwiches with as good an appetite as only a person can who after a long period of degradation, depression, and despair has suddenly found the solution to his predicament.

But on the bus, trying to think of a way to tell Anni, he was driven to distraction. He was sometimes agitated, sometimes moved by his own thoughts. At times he was shaken to the core, and then again everything seemed completely natural and self-evident.

When he arrived at the hospital, he was in a state of excitement, as if he were slightly feverish or on the way to intoxication. His eyes shone unnaturally and he walked faster, spoke and gestured more animatedly than usual.

At first Anni did not understand at all what Thor was talking about, what he meant by deceiving death's black allies and by the only solution. She was too exhausted to follow the course of his thoughts, to understand the relationship of all the words and sentences to each other. Her thoughts were concentrated on avoiding careless movements so that the sharp pain which had made her cry out before Thor's arrival would not recur.

She lay on her back without stirring, one hand on her forehead, looking at the ceiling.

"You remember that we talked about it once?" she heard Thor say.

"About what?"

"About how good it would be to die together."

"Together?"

"Yes. Hand in hand. Side by side. Anni, you don't have to die alone. We'll do it together."

"Do what? What do you mean, Thor darling?"

"I'll get some sleeping tablets, we'll take you home, and we'll leave this bad world together. Hand in hand, Anni. Just the way we said we would."

Anni drew a deep breath, closed her eyes, which had filled with tears, and bit her lip. Now she understood what Thor had meant by all his talk. No, Thor, no, she thought, overcome by pain and confusion. Not that, Thor. You can't talk that way, you can't think that way. It isn't right. It's dreadful, it's horrible, horrible.

But she said nothing. She couldn't. She was too shocked to do anything but bite her lip.

"Anni, it's our only possibility," Thor whispered. "It's a fine way to end everything, if we consider it calmly. Both of us will die soon anyway. Why not do it together, why let death separate us at the last moment. I couldn't live without you anyway after you're gone. Anni, let's think it over calmly and rationally. Don't cry, don't. At first it seems strange and frightening, but when you think of it, it's no different from going to sleep. It's just that we've been taught to fear death. That's why it seems the way it does. It's only the instinct of self-preservation that makes it seem bad and awful. But it actually isn't. We only imagine that . . ."

"Stop," Anni whispered. "Don't say anything. I can't stand to listen, I can't."

"I understand that it seems terrible to you, but if you think calmly and rationally . . ."

"Don't talk. Leave me alone."

"Anni, I have to tell you something. I went to the doctor yesterday. Do you know what he said? I have very little time left. Maybe a couple of months, at best half a year. My heart is completely worn out."

It wasn't literally true, at least the part about Thor's going to the doctor the previous day. He had resorted to this panicky lie only for Anni's sake, to make her understand that what was left of his life had no significance.

Anni said nothing. Tears began to trickle down her temples to the pillow again.

"Think of how lucky we are," Thor said. "We will both die. That's what's great about it. Everybody dies, but we can make it a victory. Think of how thankful we can be. Neither one of us will have to stay here alone to sorrow and grieve. We can arrange everything and leave worthily and happily, in a way consonant with human dignity. Do you understand what a unique opportunity we have? Don't cry, Anni dear. Be glad, be happy. You must smile."

"How can I be happy if you die," Anni sobbed, her lips trembling.

"I can't be happy either if you die," Thor explained. "But we can be happy that we'll both die, that we can die together. That's what I mean. That is happiness."

"No, Thor, no. You must live."

"Why should I live?"

"Because you must live. You have to live. A person has to live."

"But I am going to die."

"You can't."

"All people die."

"Yes, but until . . . I can't explain it now, I can't think. We'll talk about it tomorrow."

"We mustn't be afraid of death."

"We'll talk about it tomorrow. I'm so tired, so awfully tired. Put your hand on my forehead for awhile."

Thor put his hand on Anni's hot brow.

"Do you have a fever?"

"I don't know. It feels good. So soothing."

"So, Thor, my very own love, who

talks that way. It's just terrible."

"Does it seem terrible to you?"

"Let's not talk."

"Tomorrow?"

"Yes. Tomorrow then. Not now."

Although Thor understood Anni's negative position, the strength of it surprised him. But he was not discouraged. The next day, when Anni seemed a little stronger, he spoke of the subject with more enthusiasm and conviction:

"Much worse than death is the sorrow and despair it leaves behind. We have to overcome them. And that we can do only by leaving here together. Anni, we can no longer think of death as we used to. We have to bow to it. In a calm and dignified way. We have to approve of death. There is nothing else we can do. But one thing we can do, and that is the most important. We can keep death from separating us at the last moment. We have that possibility. Everything depends on us."

"But that's wrong," Anni said. "Don't you see how wrong it is, how terribly wrong your thinking is?"

"Why is it wrong?"

"Because a person has to live."

"Are you afraid of dying?"

"I am. I don't want to die, Thor. I want to live. Oh Thor, why is life like this? Why do we have to suffer all this pain? Why don't they give me something to end all this suffering? Thor, it hurts, it hurts so that I could bite through my tongue."

"Where does it hurt?"

"In my side. Everywhere. Oh, I may scream. Thor, give me your hand. I'm so sick, I'm so sick."

Anni caught Thor's hand in both of

her own and pulled herself into another position.

"I'll get the doctor," said Thor, with tears in his eyes.

"No, it's passing. You mustn't go."

"You need some medication."

"I have some. There on the table. I just haven't taken any. They make me so sleepy. Give me two of them, and a little water."

Thor handed Anni two tablets and a glass of water. After swallowing, Anni stretched out, sighing.

"Forgive me, dear."

"Why are you asking forgiveness?"

"Because I'm so weak, so miserable. I cause you nothing but worry and grief."

"You should ask forgiveness for talking like that. You make me unhappy by thinking that way."

Anni smiled weakly and reached

out her hand to Thor.

"Forgive me. I won't think that way."

"Are you sure?"

"Completely. I'm just a little unhappy sometimes."

"You have a right to be unhappy."

"I suppose so."

"Did they help?"

"They did."

"You have to take them when you feel the least bit of pain."

"I will. It's just that they make me so sleepy. I don't want to be asleep or dazed when you're here."

"Never mind that. Do you promise?"

"I promise."

IX

Two days later, Anni said:
"It's not possible."

"It's entirely possible. If we both want to."

"Do you want to?"

"I do. Do you want to?"

"I don't know."

"You have to know. We have to be fully aware of what we're doing. Two adults."

"I want to."

"Is that true?"

"It is. It is true, Thor. But they won't let me go home."

"Yes they will. I'll talk to the doctor."

Thor was a little too optimistic. The doctor he spoke to was doubtful about the matter.

"I can well understand that you would like to have her home sometimes, and that she misses home terribly. But unfortunately, it's not a simple matter. Your wife needs constant daily care. It isn't easy to arrange that at home."

"I would take care of her."

"Yes, yes, I don't doubt that at all. But the procedure is very complicated and requires being in a hospital. And doesn't it seem right and reasonable to you that she get the best possible proper care — till the end."

"Yes, but . . ."

"I think so too. So won't we agree to her staying here at least temporarily, even though I can very well understand your wishes. It's certainly best for her. And above all we must think of her. Isn't that true? But come and see her often. Think and be grateful for every day you can still keep her. Make her remaining days as happy and beautiful as possible, won't you?"

"Yes."

Thor understood that it was no use to argue with the doctor. But this small setback did not discourage him. It made him all the more determined."

"I'll just take you home," he said to Anni.

"But if they stop you?"

"We'll sneak out. Without anyone's noticing. Right at the beginning of visiting hours. We'll take a taxi home."

"A taxi?"

"We don't have to think about money any more. Isn't that a fine thing too. We could even hire a plane if we wanted to."

They looked at one another in silence like two people who share an exciting secret. In their thoughts they were already home in their own beds, hand in hand, side by side. In part it still seemed like play, an enchanting dream, both enticing and fearful.

"Oh, my very own love," Anni whispered, pressing Thor's hand to her cheek. "What exactly are we planning, what do we intend to do?"

"To cheat death," said Thor.

X

Having heard Thor's partly con-trived, partly true story of his troublesome sleeplessness, and having checked him over superficially, the Helsinki physician — the sixth in three days — asked:

"Have you ever taken sleeping pills before?"

"Oh yes," said Thor, taking an old, crumpled prescription from his wallet. "This kind. I would be happy if the doctor could prescribe the same kind for me. They suit me fine."

The doctor turned the prescription over in his hand and pursed his lips.

"They're quite strong. Suppose I write up twenty tablets?"

"Excuse me, but could I have a little more?"

"Thirty?"

"Forty. So that I wouldn't need another prescription so soon."

The doctor began to study the prescription again and pursed his lips.

"Well, I suppose I'll write one up for forty," he said, taking a prescription booklet from a desk drawer. "Yes, forty. I think you'll get to sleep with them. There seems to be something in your heart. It would be worth having it checked."

"Yes."

"And you mustn't eat these like bread. Only one tablet when you really

need it. Not every night. So, forty tablets. The effect of one will last longer
than you think. Yes, exactly so. And
go and have that heart of yours
checked. There may be some little
thing wrong with it. Well then, that's
it. Forty tablets. One tablet as needed.
Be so good."

"Thank you. How much do . . ."

"Twenty-five *markkas*."

Thor paid him, got a receipt, and left
feeling satisfied, with a sixth prescription in his pocket. He had somewhat
the same feeling as when he had paid
the last installment on the apartment.
The prescriptions somehow reminded
him of tickets, and the drugstores of
travel agencies.

To find another drugstore — he had
already visited several of the downtown ones — he took a taxi, asked the
cabby to drive over Longbridge to the

Söörna district. When they came to the Cape Paddock market, he asked the driver if there were any drugstores nearby.

The driver began to peer out the window.

"There's one at least."

"Drive over to it."

Having bought the sleeping tablets, Thor went to the hospital in the same taxi. When he paid the fare and was just about to get up, a sudden spasm of pain forced him back onto the seat.

"Are you ill?"

"No," Thor mumbled, "I'm just a little tired. It'll pass. Just a second . . . I'll go right away . . ."

"There's no hurry. Just take it easy. Luckily we're in front of a hospital."

Thor got the heart medication out of his pocket and put a pill into his mouth. It has to pass, he thought fearfully. There's no time to be sick now. I have to be strong. Stronger than ever.

"Should I get someone to take care of you?" asked the driver.

"It isn't necessary. I'm better already."

"Was it something with your heart?"

"No."

"You're all sweaty."

"It's the warm weather. That's what it's from."

"Still, maybe I should get someone . . ."

"No thank you. It's over already. I'm going now . . . thanks for the ride."

Thor got up carefully. The pain had slackened. The driver rushed out of the cab to help him.

"Are you sure you're all right?"

"Yes, I'm fine. Thank you."

"Lucky it happened in front of a hospital. They'll be sure to give you some medication."

"I'm sure they will. So long."

"So long."

Walking carefully, Thor went through the hospital door. His chest and diaphragm still felt sore, but the sharp pain was gone. It has to be soon, he thought. He couldn't delay, couldn't take any risks. He couldn't get sick, he couldn't wind up in a hospital. All would be lost then. As soon as possible. Maybe on Sunday already. Next Sunday. Sunday would be a good day.

"Sunday?" Anni whispered.

"Yes. What do you think?"

"I don't know."

"It has to happen soon. We have to act quickly so that nothing will happen . . . so that we won't run into any problems." Thor took a packet of sleeping tablets from his pocket and showed it to Anni in the shelter of his cupped hand.

"Look."

Anni turned away and put her hand to her forehead.

"How many are there?"

"Forty. Altogether we have two hundred and ten. Over a hundred for each of us. That's more than enough."

"Put them away."

"Of course." Nonplussed at the tone of her voice, Thor thrust the sleeping tablets he had been so proud of back into his pocket.

"What's the matter?"

"Nothing."

"Does it hurt again?"

"No. Forgive me."

"Why?"

"For being like this. Hold my hand."

Thor took Anni's hand in his and patted it gently.

"Are you afraid?"

"I don't know. Maybe."

"There's nothing to be afraid of."

"I know, but I can't help it. Forgive me for being like this. I don't think I can do it. I've been thinking that it still isn't right. Oh Thor dear, I feel so bad for being like this. I don't know what's wrong with me. I don't understand myself."

"You don't want to?"

"I want to. It's not that. I want to as much as you do. But something keeps bothering me all the time . . . I can't explain it . . . I just have the feeling that it's wrong, somehow terribly wrong."

"I understand. I have the same feeling sometimes. It's completely natural. It comes from having been taught to see it that way. But it isn't so. We only imagine that there is something wrong and culpable in it."

"Yes, but what can I do?"

"Because we see it that way?"

"Yes."

"We just have to try to think of the matter rationally and practically. We have to understand that we have an absolute right to do so, that nothing can condemn us for doing so except our own prejudices."

"I've even thought that you might regret it."

"I?"

"Yes."

"I won't regret it. Not under any circumstances. It's the finest thing we can get out of life. To leave here together. It's a great thing, rightly considered. But I have no right to influence you too much. You have to think the matter through and through yourself and come to your own decision."

"It's so strange. I want it, it's the most

beautiful idea in the world to me, and yet . . . I don't know, I simply don't know what is right."

"You have to think it over carefully. From every angle. And then come to a decision. One or the other. Isn't that so? We both have to be fully conscious, fully clear about what we're doing. Only then can we do it as free people."

"I will think it over," promised Anni.

When Thor came to the hospital the next day, Thursday, Anni had made a decision.

"We'll do it."

"Are you completely sure of yourself?"

"I am. Completely sure. I thought about it the whole night. We'll do it, Thor."

"You're not afraid?"

"No. It's the best thing that can happen to me."

"That can happen to us."

"Yes, love. That can happen to us. We'll go together, in beauty and dignity, in a way worthy of human beings. Together we'll deceive death."

"On Sunday?"

"On Sunday."

"Your thumb on it?"

"My thumb on it."

They pressed their thumbs together and held them there for a long time, looking each other in the eyes with a smile on their lips.

XI

n Friday, Thor did not make it to the hospital. He spent the whole morning organizing his papers. Some he threw away, but all the more important papers and documents, such as his share in the apartment, in the telephone co-op, his bankbooks, his pension and tax receipts he put into a manila envelope and took to a safe-deposit box at the bank. Already in it were his and Anni's reciprocal wills, a pair of old bankbooks, and a cancelled loan agreement. According to the will, they inherited from each other, and in case both of them died, the property would go to their nearest living relative, a nephew.

He accomplished all these tasks calmly and decisively, although a blind instinct to live did its best to make him hesitate. The last enticements and promises of deceitful life, reinforced and beautified by many memories from the life he had lived, had only a momentary and passing effect on him. They were merely dreams. For a moment he would sink into thought, feel an inexplicable longing brush his soul, but a gentle sigh or a melancholy smile was sufficient to re-establish the truth.

After returning from the bank, he felt a slight pang in his breast, so slight that earlier he would have paid no attention to it. Now he stopped at once, put a pill into his mouth, and checked his pulse. He could no longer run the slightest risk.

In the evening, Thor wrote three letters. One was addressed to his nephew, and in it he bade him a beautiful goodbye:

You've always been like a child of our own. When you were little, you used to visit us often. Do you still remember those days? It's many years since we last saw you. We heard that you'd got married. We were very happy to hear it, even though you're not quite a graybeard yet. All our best and much good luck to you and your wife.

When you get this letter, your

Aunt Anni and I will already have left this world. I believe you will adjust to this news in an understanding way. We left of our own free will, fully conscious and with all our faculties intact. We were both gravely ill and had little time left. Our lives have been happy up to this point. We have loved each other. We did not want death to separate us at the last moment.

Death is a human being's worst enemy. It leaves behind only sorrow, grief, and despair. We intend to play a little trick on that gloomy old gentleman. We are leaving here as happily as we have lived. I am sure you will understand.

You will be our heir. All our papers are in the savings bank here, and I urge you to get in touch with its president. He's sure to help you with the inventory and other matters, because he's a lawyer.

If you want to put an obituary in the paper, it should say that we left the world happily and in a way accordant with human dignity. We hope that the following lines will appear in the lower corner of the notice:

> *See in my yard*
> *there is a tree.*
> *It always blooms in*
> *June.*

Both Aunt Anni and I have always loved this song, and we would be happy if these words would take the place of the usual snatch of hymn in the obituary.

I should write something else,

but I don't remember what it was. It can hardly be anything important. Many regards and all our best to you and your wife. Live happy.

Your uncle Thor

Having finished the letters — one to the hospital and the other to the sheriff — Thor addressed the envelopes, put in the letters, and pasted on the stamps.

He decided to mail them on Sunday so they would arrive on Monday at the earliest.

124

XII

On Saturday, at Thor's stubborn insistence, the super's wife came once more to clean the apartment. She was annoyed and reluctant; she had enough to do in her own home on Saturday, nor was she at all pleased at Thor's efforts to supervise the cleaning the whole time and give her advice and directions.

"There's still dust on the window sill," he would say.

"I'll wipe it, I'll wipe it, when I get to it."

"The refrigerator has to be washed too."

"I'll wash it. If the gentleman would just stay out of my way."

"Is the bathroom in shape?"

"It is, it is."

Thor went to check. It did seem all right. There was no dust on his finger after he ran it across the top of the cabinet.

The super's wife had to sacrifice three hours of her Saturday before the apartment was sufficiently clean and neat in Thor's eyes.

"It's fine now," he said, bending over to pick up a small piece of white thread that had stuck to the rug. "Isn't it beginning to look shipshape?"

"Well is it then?"

"Yes. I'll pay for everything now."

"Your wife will pay me later."

"No, she asked me to pay."

"Well, in that case . . ."

"How much is it altogether?"

The woman counted on her fingers.

"Forty-five *markkas* all told. Or is that too much?"

Thor handed her sixty *markkas*.

"Be so good. That's it exactly."

"No, this is too much."

"No it isn't."

"Well, thank you very much. Shall I come again on Monday?"

"It's not necessary."

"The gentleman will let me know?"

"Yes."

"Goodbye. My regards to your wife."

"Thank you."

When the woman had left, Thor put out fresh towels in the kitchen and bathroom. Then he took four sheets and the pillowcases that went with them from the linen closet, carried them into the bedroom, and began to make the beds over again.

Taking off the old sheets, he spread the new ones in their place. They were Anni's guest sheets, huge things, made of the finest linen, and ironed till they shone. The top sheets had a lace edging and a broad pink hem binding with Anni's name embroidered in it. The pillowcases bore the same decoration.

With the sheets folded down a half-meter over the covers and with the matching pillowcases, the bedroom looked different — fine and ceremonial.

Having put the old sheets and pillowcases into the plastic laundry basket in the bathroom closet, Thor left the apartment. He went to the florist on Market Street where he had often bought flowers for Anni. Earlier he had been satisfied with one bunch, but now he chose several.

"Are all these flowers for your wife?" wondered the florist — a woman who wore glasses and laughed easily — when Thor had bought a sizable number of five different flowers: roses, carnations, irises, narcissus, and lily-of-the-valley.

"Yes they are. And I'll take some of those flowers there. What are they?"

"These are violets."

"Right. I'll take them too."

"All of them?"

"Yes."

"Thank you so much."

The florist wrapped the violets eagerly into a paper. That made it six packages.

"Your wife will really be happy when she sees all these flowers," she said in awe. "She's sure to be happy. And such beautiful flowers. Will you even be able to carry them all? I can get my daughter to help."

"I can manage very well."

"Are you sure?"

"Yes. How much do they cost?"

"One minute. I really have to figure it out on paper. The florist tore off a piece of wrapping paper and began hastily to scribble numbers on it. "Oh my, it comes to eighty-four markkas. The roses are so expensive and there are quite a lot of them, but let's make it an even eighty markkas."

Thor paid and the woman hung packages of flowers from his fingers.

"Can you really carry all of them now?"

"I'm positive I can."

"Should we fasten the last one to this button?"

"That will be good."

The florist hung the package of violets onto a button of Thor's poplin coat.

"There. Now they'll go easily. I hear that your wife is getting better. She's sure to get completely well now when she gets so awfully many gorgeous flowers. Tell her awfully many regards from me. I've always admired the flowers on her balcony so much. They turn out so incredibly well. I sometimes actually stop to look and enjoy them. They are so beautiful. Remember to give her all my best regards. Many, many heartfelt greetings and wishes for a speedy recovery."

"I'll tell her. Thank you very much. I'll see you."

"Thank you so very much."

Thor left through the open door of the flower shop with the florist's happy smile to send him off and walked home across the market square.

Climbing onto a chair, he found in an upper kitchen cabinet five different kinds of vases and two milk pitchers decorated with roses and violets that he remembered Anni's having used as vases.

Having half-filled the vases and pitchers with water, he proceeded to set the flowers into them, and succeeded in producing seven such brilliant and magnificent flower arrangements that he himself was astonished. The left-over flowers he put into two beer tankards.

He carried the roses, which filled two large vases, to the night table in the bedroom. The lilies-of-the-valley he put on the table made from an old sewing machine. The rest of the flowers he placed around the living room and kitchen.

The glow of color and the smell of the flowers was dizzying. Thor went to draw the curtains further back so that the sun could shine in better. His hands were still raised, gripping the curtains, when he felt a blow as if a horse had kicked the center of his chest. The bright sunlight flashed in his eyes, the market square spun around, and then everything dimmed. He curled up and sank first to his knees and then to one side on the floor.

"Not yet," he whimpered aloud. "Not yet. I can't die. I can't get sick. Anni, wait for me. Anni, Anni . . ."

The pain was so severe that he could not get his hand into the pocket where the pills were. He saw the violets on the coffee table, the square formed by sunlight on the wall behind them. His panic was overwhelming. He was not religious, he had not often prayed, but now a despairing plea burst from his lips.

"Help me, God, give me one more day. For Anni's sake. Have mercy on me."

Who can say if God heard Thor's plea or if his desire to cheat death was actually stronger than death itself? In any case, he recovered from the attack, his fourth and last blood clot.

For two hours, Thor did not dare move from the sofa he managed to crawl to after the pain had begun to subside. When he finally rose carefully to his feet, probed his chest with his hand, took a few steps, and found that everything seemed all right again, standing there in the middle of the living room surrounded by sunlight and flowers on the day before starting out on his last journey, he looked humbly upward and whispered to someone in whose existence he did not believe:

"Thanks."

XIII

In the morning as he got out of bed after a few hours of sleep, Thor was clearly conscious of one thing: he had awakened from sleep for the last time.

Shaving in the bathroom, he had the same thought: his last shave.

Then he made his bed, dressed, and prepared the tea, knowing that he was doing all this for the last time.

Having drunk the tea and eaten two slices of French bread, he went into the living room and drew back the curtains.

It was raining. It was the first Sunday in September. The market square, bathed by the warm rain, was gray and empty. A single car drove by on the far side, its windshield wipers working slowly.

"Don't cry," Thor muttered aloud, glancing at the cloudy sky. "I won't cry either. It's a happy and sunny day."

And in truth, behind the buildings to the left, blue openings were visible through gaps in the clouds. They grew larger and larger, and when Thor went out an hour later on his last walk, as far as the beach pavilion, a light wind had cleared the clouds from the whole western half of the sky and the sun shone unhindered on the rain-fresh town.

The church bells were beginning to

ring when Thor returned home.

He took the sleeping tablets out of the kitchen cabinet where he had stored them and divided them one by one into two small glass bowls which Anni had used as dessert dishes.

He threw the empty medicine jars into a garbage bag which he dropped into the garbage chute on the drying balcony.

He took the glass bowls into the bedroom and put them on the night table beside the roses.

He put the three letters from on top of the cabinet in the living room into his breast pocket.

Then he rested on the sofa for over an hour, thinking of Anni and their life together, which was to end in a few hours.

He felt no further hesitation, but only a faint nostalgia, perhaps the same kind as emigrants feel when they

prepare to leave their familiar home-
land forever.

It was not indifference, much less
apathy. When the time came to order
a car and driver, he was definite and
businesslike, and especially aware of
the deed's significance. Every movement of his finger on the dial was
weighty and final, and when he got in
— with Anni's ulster, shoes and stockings in his lap — and the car started
off, he knew that the last journey had
begun.

Soon, even before he was aware, he
was sitting beside Anni's bed. He took
two tablets from the table and gave
them to Anni, who swallowed them
without saying anything.

"Are you ready?"

"I am."

"Do you think you can walk?"

"I'll try."

Thor glanced behind him. There

were already visitors around the four beds although it was still five minutes till visiting hours. A man and woman came in through the door. The woman had a bunch of flowers in her hand. They went to the patient opposite Thor and Anni. Not a single nurse was in sight.

"Let's go."

Anni sat up. She held on to Thor's hand for support and shifted first one foot and then the other from the bed. Every one of her movements was slow and cautious. Having gotten to a standing position on the floor, she hung on to Thor with both hands, swaying back and forth.

"I'm dizzy," she whispered. Her eyes were closed and her head drooped. "I have to sit down."

She sank to a sitting position on the edge of the bed, supported by Thor.

"It will pass," Thor whispered.

"How can a person get so weak," Anni sighed. "My pocketbook is there. We mustn't forget it."

"I'll take it. Shall we try again?"

"I don't know if I can."

"Yes you can. Hold on to me."

Anni stood up slowly. She managed to thrust her feet into a pair of hospital slippers.

"How does it feel?"

"A little better. Let's go, darling. But not too fast."

They began a slow and painful progress toward the door. Anni had wrapped her arm around Thor's neck and he had to carry half her weight. The soft whispers around the beds ceased and everyone watched Thor and Anni's departure for awhile.

They were successful in reaching the hallway. Thor looked in both directions. No one wearing white was to be seen.

"Can you make it?"

"Yes."

They started off toward the elevator, stopping often to rest. A young attendant wearing glasses entered the hallway and walked toward them with a pack of patients' cards in her hand. As she passed them, a kindly smile crossed her face.

"Could that have been . . . ?"

"No. A total stranger."

When they stepped into the elevator, Anni was so exhausted by the effort of walking that she wrapped both arms around Thor's neck and held on to keep from falling.

"I'm so dizzy, so dizzy."

"A short distance more. We'll soon be in the car."

"Yes, love."

"Just hold on tight."

"Yes."

In the lobby there were patients sitting with their relatives, and a pair of doctors walked by, but they paid no attention to the old couple, a man in a poplin coat and a woman in a hospital morning coat who approached the glass outer door painfully, step by step, the woman with her eyes shut and her head pressed against her husband's shoulder.

Seeing them coming, the rental driver got up and rushed toward them. He caught Anni's other arm and helped Thor get her into the car.

"That was some trip," said Anni, totally exhausted. "I couldn't have taken another step."

"I have your shoes and stockings," said Thor.

"Later dear. Not now. I can't."

"And your coat? Will you put this on?"

"Later then. Not now."

Thor spread the ulster over Anni's legs and sat down beside her. Anni pressed her cheek against his shoulder. The automobile started off.

"Stop by a mailbox," Thor said to the driver.

In the hospital, Anni's absence was noted as soon as visiting hours were over. The section doctor to whom two worried attendants came to report the matter said:

"I don't know if there is a reason for us to do anything. The old man has been so terribly lonesome for his wife and she's been just as terribly homesick. She told me about it. Why don't we let them spend this Sunday together? In their own home. It may mean a lot to them. More than we can

144

guess. We're not policemen. Or are we? What are you smiling at, girls? Do you have a better suggestion?"

"We don't," the oldest of them said. "We can assure you, doctor, that we don't have a better suggestion."

XIV

Anni stood in the middle of the living room. She was staggering with weariness, but she no longer felt it.

"Is it true? Are we really here again?"

"We are here."

"My goodness, what a heap of flowers!"

"I bought a few flowers. Sit here and rest."

"Let me look, let me enjoy this. It's

so nice here, so neat."

"The super's wife was here to clean yesterday."

"I can see that. Oh Thor, you make me so happy. Don't complain if I cry. I thought I would never see our home again. I have to see the balcony flowers too. How are they doing?"

"Very well."

Anni was able to go to the balcony on her own. Seeing her home, the familiar objects and atmosphere had invigorated her to that extent. Coming back from the balcony with tears in her eyes, she went into the kitchen, caressed the counter with her hand, and asked Thor to open the cabinet doors so that she could once more see all the glassware and china.

"Thank you. You can close them now."

They went back into the living

room and sat on the sofa with their arms around each other.

"Darling . . ."

"Yes?"

"It's beautiful to be home."

"It is."

"What are you thinking of?"

"All kinds of things."

"Of that?"

"That too."

"I'm not afraid of it any more."

"Neither am I."

"Isn't it amazing to think . . ."

"It is. Yesterday I read a good thought on death. It's from Socrates' Apology, when he was condemned to die."

"Where did you read it?"

"In the book *Thoughts for the Ages*."

"Read it to me when we go to sleep."

"I will."

"When will we go?"

"When you want to."

"I would be ready for bed right now."

"Are you tired?"

"Quite a bit. The trip exhausted me."

"Let's go to sleep."

"Let's."

On thousands of evenings, they had spoken of going to sleep in the same way, often used those same words. On thousands of evenings they had gone into the bedroom, climbed into bed, said goodnight to one another, and sunk into unconsciousness.

And now, when they were doing it all for the last time? Was the gap between this and all the previous evenings so immeasurable, so unbridgeable? Or was it infinitesimally small, insignificant?

Let him who can answer the question. Anyone still firmly in the grasp of life cannot think of the matter objectively.

Life could not have given Thor a greater gift than Anni's bedazzlement at the roses, lilies-of-the-valley, and the beautifully made beds. Anni realized it and exaggerated her delight just a little as she sat on the edge of the bed.

"Darling, this isn't true. It's a fairytale."

"So it is."

"What a heavenly fragrance. How did you manage all this?"

"I just went to the florist. Does it look good?"

"My dear love, I can't believe my eyes."

"They are the finest roses they had."

"I can see that. You've even changed the sheets. Where did you find these?"

"In the closet. Don't they go well?"

"They do. I'm glad you changed them."

"Our best sheets."

"They are. But I will go to bed right now. I'm so tired, so unbelievably tired. Darling, won't you get my own nightgown. The blue one."

"Yes. Where is it?"

"In the hall closet. Where the sheets were. Somewhere on the bottom shelf."

Thor found the nightgown. He helped Anni take off the hospital clothing and put on the nightgown.

"How lovely," Anni sighed as Thor covered her in bed. "How perfectly lovely. In my own bed wearing my own nightgown. It's a lovely feeling."

"I know."

"Aren't you coming to bed?"

"Right away. I just thought I would smoke a cigarette."

"Go ahead, dear."

Then Anni noticed the glass bowl on the night table.

"Are those the . . . ?"

"They are."

"Kiss me."

As he smoked the cigarette in the living room, it seemed strangely unreal to Thor that it should be his last. A few times earlier he had smoked his last cigarette in an effort to quit, but deep down he had never believed it to be actually the last. Nor could he really believe it now. In a way he was right, for when he stubbed out the cigarette in the ash tray, he lighted another, as if to do justice to his unbelief and his craving for nicotine, whose reach exceeded the conceptual limits of death.

It was his last cigarette, but he no longer thought about that.

Having undressed and put on his

best pajamas, he got two glasses of water from the kitchen, set them on the night table, and lay down beside Anni.

Her hand searched out his.

"My love."

"Yes darling. Here we are again."

"You promised to read something to me."

"That's true. I forgot."

Thor fetched the book from the living room and read the following passage from it to Anni:

Death has to be one of two things: either it is nothing at all, and the dead person knows nothing, or it is, as they used to say of old, some kind of move, the moving of the soul from this place to another. If death ends all knowledge, so that it is like a deep and dreamless sleep, then death is a marvelous victory. Then all eternity is just one night. If again death is some kind of migration from this place to another, and if what they say is true, that all the dead are there, can one then think of a greater happiness, my honored judges? For if we go to the realm of Hades and are freed there from those who call themselves judges, and find in their place right-thinking judges and the other heroes — wouldn't it be a delightful journey? What wouldn't you give to meet Orpheus and Musaeus and Hesiod and Homer!

"Thank you for reading it to me," said Anni.

"They were Socrates' thoughts just before he drank the glass of poison."

"Which do you believe?"

"I don't know. Nor did Socrates either. In the end, it doesn't mean anything."

"He died peacefully?"

"Peacefully and with dignity. Shall we turn on the radio?"

"Let's."

A familiar hit song was playing.

Could there be a lovelier day?
A lovelier morning than this?
With my love at my side
O so quiet and close
Is anything lovelier than this?

"It's that song."

"So it is."

"I've always liked it."

"It's a good song."

"Who sings it?"

"I don't remember. Anni . . ."

"Yes love . . ."

"There's so much I want to say to you, so much left unsaid."

"You've said it just by being."

"I love you. I've always loved you."

"I know, Thor. I've always loved you too. You are my only one, my very own."

"I want to thank you for everything, for all those years together, but I can't find the right words. I don't know how to tell you everything I feel."

"You've said it already. It couldn't be said more beautifully. I want to thank you too. For everything. Thank you, Thor, for our lovely life together. And I can't believe that everything will end even now. Oh my dear, come closer, put your arms around me. I want to be very close to you, a part of you. That's exactly right, that's good."

They lay quietly looking at each other. The radio was on softly; someone sang of a longing for the plains of the North.

"When shall we take them?"

"When you feel it's . . ."

"It has to happen before I fall asleep."

"Yes. You have to tell me before that."

"I feel . . . my eyes are closing."

"Are you getting sleepy?"

"I am. So awfully. I don't know if I can stay awake any longer."

"We have to do it."

"Yes dear. Or maybe this tired spell will pass if I . . ."

"Anni, are you asleep?"

"No."

"We have to do it now."

"Yes, love. We'll do it now."

Anni, who had been falling asleep, raised herself on her elbows and took a glass bowl from the table first.

"Do I have to take them all?"

"At least half. Drink water with them."

They began to take the tablets, four or five at a time, washing them down with water. At this point, everything was easier than they could have imagined in advance. They did not think about death or the life beyond, nor even of one another at that moment. All their attention was concentrated on the white tablets and the act of swallowing them.

Then they put the bowls back on the night table and settled down to rest face to face with their arms around each other.

"Like bread," Thor smiled.

"What, love?"

"The doctor said not to eat them like bread."

"Did he say that?"

"He did. Do you feel good?"

"I do. Do you?"

"Very good. We cheated death, Anni."

"Yes, my very own love. I think I'll sleep now. Good night, my own most beloved."

"Good night my love. Sleep well, won't you?"

"I will. And you too. We've left the radio on."

"Let it play."

SEE IN MY YARD
THERE IS A TREE.
IT ALWAYS BLOOMS IN
JUNE.

About the Author

TAUNO YLIRUUSI has been a free-lance writer since 1968. He is one of the few contemporary Finnish writers to have won international recognition for his work.

From the beginning, a career in writing was a natural course for Yliruusi to follow. Both his mother and his father were editors. His father was also a lawyer active in politics, which may have influenced his choice of studies at the University of Helsinki, where he opted for a master's degree in political science instead of literature, that usual choice of aspiring writers.

Following commencement and army service, Yliruusi worked as editor or administrator in such diverse organizations as the Finnish League of Private Entrepreneurs, the Finnish

Information Agency, Finnish television, the Finnish United Nations Organization, private companies and a taxpayers' league. He has served on boards of many literary groups.

Although primarily a dramatist, Tauno Yliruusi is a highly versatile writer. In addition to plays, he has some twenty books to his credit, including both prose and poetry. He has contributed columns and humorous sketches to many newspapers and magazines under different pen names. His works range from novels and parodies of crime fiction to short stories and pamphlets. Many of his plays have gained recognition abroad. Six have appeared in Modern International Drama, published by the Max Reinhardt Archives of the State University of New York at Binghamton. A few have been presented in college theaters in the United States.

Translations of "Murder for Fun," Yliruusi's parody of suspense novels, have been broadcast frequently in Britain, Canada, Germany, Holland, Belgium, Switzerland and Czechoslovakia, and by the *Comédie Française* as one of its radio series. All told, his works have been performed in fifteen languages in twenty-five countries. *Hand in Hand* is the first of his novels to be published in the United States.

Mr. Yliruusi lives with his wife near Helsinki.